SERIES CANA

NINE LIVES
by Prem Omkaro

The cabin was quiet. Every awful thing that had happened since they caught me came crowding into my mind. I didn't want to believe what was happening. I just wanted to close my eyes, and when I opened them again to be somewhere else—somewhere safe.

   I started to cry. *Please God,* I prayed, *just get me out of this, and I'll never snoop again. I promise.*

SERIES CANADA

PREM OMKARO

NINE LIVES

Maxwell Macmillan Canada

Copyright © 1988 by Maxwell Macmillan Canada Inc. All rights reserved. No part of this book may be reproduced or transmitted in any form or by any means, electronic or mechanical, including photocopying, recording, or by any information storage and retrieval system, without permission in writing from the Publisher.

Maxwell Macmillan Canada
1200 Eglinton Ave. East, Suite 200
Don Mills, Ontario M3C 3N1

ISBN 02-953542-5

General Editor: Paul Kropp
Series Editor: Sandra Gulland
Designer: Brant Cowie
Illustrator: Marilyn Mets
Cover Photograph: Paterson Photographic

3 4 5 6 93 92 91
Printed and bound in Canada.

Canadian Cataloguing in Publication Data

Omkaro, Prem, 1948–
  Nine Lives

(Series Canada)

ISBN 02-953542-5

I. Title   II. Series.

PS8579.M53N55 1988   jC813´.54   C88-094800-0
PZ7.053Ni 1988

CONTENTS

CHAPTER 1
7
CHAPTER 2
14
CHAPTER 3
23
CHAPTER 4
33
CHAPTER 5
41
CHAPTER 6
48
CHAPTER 7
55
CHAPTER 8
60
CHAPTER 9
66
CHAPTER 10
77

CHAPTER

Quickly I looked under a sofa cushion. Dust puffed up in my face. I pinched my nose to keep from sneezing and slipped my other hand down the side of the sofa. Yuck! An apple core, some pennies, and a piece of broken pencil.

The Cranks were real slobs. There were empty beer cans on the sofa and floor. There were newspapers all over the place. The full ashtrays were gross and the place smelled like old cigarette smoke.

This was the first time I had been in their cabin alone. The first four weeks they were always there when I cleaned.

The Cranks would nag and bug each other while I took out the garbage. Sometimes they made me think of the way my brother and I carried on.

It was strange the way they spent so much time in their cabin, even in this heat wave. All the other guests at the lodge went outside, water skied, or went down to the beach. But the Cranks just sat around arguing. I didn't know why they even came up here. Auberge du Lac was filled with young couples from Montreal, families with kids, and lots of American tourists. The Cranks just didn't fit in.

I opened the drawer of a small table and looked inside. All I found were old comics and blank paper.

Stop snooping, Cat! I told myself, closing the drawer. I had been hired to clean the cabins here at the lodge—not to snoop through them! But I just couldn't help myself. Whenever I got a chance, I read letters, looked under beds, or peeked into drawers.

I guess that's why I got the nickname "Cat." My real name is Cathy, but my mom and dad have called me Cat ever since I was a kid. "You're as curious as a cat," my dad would tell me. "It's going to get you in big trouble one of these days. You're lucky a cat has nine lives instead of one."

And Dad was right. I am curious. I almost got kicked out of school because of it. The last week, I was caught going through some papers on my French teacher's desk. How could I know that our exam was in the pile?

Of course, my parents freaked out, and almost made me stay home for the summer. Only some heavy-duty begging had saved the day.

I would have died if they made me give up this job at the lodge. Cleaning cabins and waiting on tables may not sound all that great, but it beats being a waitress in Lachine all summer. Besides, I was sixteen and this was my first chance to be away from home on my own. And it was fun sharing a cabin with the other kids and hanging out with them on the beach.

I just wish that cleaning cabins didn't make it so easy to snoop, I thought. But here I was—doing it again.

I headed for the bedroom, not ready to

give up. I looked under the mattress, but found nothing. Then I shook the suitcases under the bed. Empty. I went through the pockets of the clothes hanging in the closet. Zip. Pretty boring so far.

But I had saved the best for last. Dressers often had the juicy stuff—pictures, letters, old copies of *Penthouse*.

I started to pull open a drawer—and stopped. Weird noises were coming from the other room—thumping sounds.

I knew I had locked the door to the cabin, so I tiptoed over to the doorway between the two rooms and peeked into the other room.

It was only a bird. Somehow it had got in and was banging wildly against the window and screens. The bird was so scared I thought it would break through the glass. As quick as I could, I took the key out of my shorts and unlocked the door. Then I ran around behind the bird, waving my arms so it would fly outside.

I locked the door again and put the key back in my pocket. I wondered how the bird had got in. Except for the big picture window looking out on the lake, the rest of the small windows were screened.

Could the bird have come down the chimney of the brick fireplace? Going over to it, I knelt down and looked up inside. I could see light. A metal plate up in the chimney was half open, and there was plenty of room for a bird to squeeze through. Maybe that explained it.

That was when I noticed something strange about the fireplace. A giant pile of ashes filled the grate, as if a lot of paper had been burned there.

Why would anyone light a fire in this hot weather? I wondered. And if the Cranks wanted to get rid of some paper, why didn't they just throw it in the garbage?

There was one bit of half-burned paper left. Picking it up very slowly so it wouldn't fall apart, I stared at it. The only letters I could make out were "ADA" and then "SAV" and then "BON." The rest was burned out.

What had it said? Why had it been burned? I knelt on the floor by the fireplace thinking about the whole thing. I knew I should get back to cleaning and get out of there, but this made me really curious.

I decided to take one last look through the dresser. Back in the bedroom, I slid open the top right-hand drawer—just underwear, nylons, and socks. I felt through them carefully so the Cranks wouldn't know they had been touched. But there was nothing else.

I closed the drawer and opened the one next to it—more underwear and socks. As I moved a pair of socks, I heard a crackle.

Socks don't crackle!

Holding my breath, I unrolled the socks. A key and a folded piece of newspaper dropped into my palm.

"All right!" I whispered out loud.

I put the key down on the dresser and started to unfold the paper, but then, for the second time, I stopped dead. I heard voices close by—two people arguing, a man and a woman. The Cranks! It sounded like they were right outside the cabin.

I stood there trapped, not moving.

Then I heard a key, turning in the lock of the cabin door.

CHAPTER 2

Fear ripped through me—and with the fear came the will to move.

Shaking, I pushed the key and paper back into the socks. I rolled up the socks, put them in their place, and quietly closed the drawer. I wiped my sweaty palms on the back of my shorts.

The door slammed shut in the other room. "I'm not going on that stupid boat tour," said Mr. Crank. "I'm sick of you telling me what to do."

"And I'm tired of being stuck inside this cabin day after day," Mrs. Crank told him. "We haven't budged for a month and

I'm going nuts. Besides, it's got to look funny. People are going to wonder what we're doing here if we don't go out."

I was in a panic. I shouldn't be listening to this. I should have finished my cleaning a half hour ago and gotten out of there.

I had to be quick. Grabbing the wastebasket beside the bed, I walked into the other room. "Hi, Mr. and Mrs. Crank," I said, as simply as I could, emptying the trash into a green garbage bag.

Were they ever surprised to see me. Like a couple of dummies in a store window, they just stood there, not moving at all. They were about the same height, had the same square build and the same short blonde hair, carbon copies of each other.

I took the wastebasket back into the bedroom and sat it on the floor beside the bed. There was dead silence in the cabin.

"What are you doing here?" Mrs. Crank snapped as I came back into the main room.

"I know I'm late today, but I'll be done cleaning in a few minutes," I mumbled.

"The door was locked," she said. "Why?"

"Oh . . . sorry," I said, trying to make it

sound like I was surprised. "I guess I must have locked it behind me without thinking. I'll only be a few more minutes."

"Just take your things and get out," Mrs. Crank ordered.

I quickly grabbed my mop and broom and left. I walked back to the main lodge, following the dirt road that ran behind the cabins. I was really glad to be out of there. That had been a little too close and it left me shaking.

I thought about what the Cranks had said, and it sure sounded strange to me. What did Mrs. Crank mean about it looking funny?

I had to talk to somebody, and of course, I thought of Jean-Luc. He waited on tables and helped M. Fontaine, the owner of the resort.

Jean-Luc had become my best friend over the summer. We had met at the beginning of the season and liked each other right away. But not like a girlfriend and boyfriend would. Jean-Luc just wasn't my type, or so I thought at first. But he was fun to be with and he always made me laugh and feel good. Lately I wished we could be more than just friends, but I didn't know how to change things. Maybe I wasn't *his* type.

I wondered if Jean-Luc was back from town. During breakfast he had told me he was going with M. Fontaine to Knowlton, a little town about a fifteen-minute drive from the resort.

When I reached the main lodge I put my supplies back in a small wooden shed. Beside it, in Mme. Fontaine's office, I hung up my keys to the cabins on a pegboard.

Mme. Fontaine looked up from her desk and said, "Mon Dieu! You're late this

morning, Cathy. Are we giving you too much work to do?"

"No," I said, trying to smile, "but I was a little late getting started." I couldn't tell her the truth—that I was late because I had been snooping. "Are M. Fontaine and Jean-Luc back from town?" I asked her.

"Not yet, but I'm glad you reminded me," Mme. Fontaine said. "They might not be back in time for the start of lunch. Would you see that Jean-Luc's tables are looked after?"

"Sure, the kids and I will take care of them," I answered. Then I left the office, letting the screen door bang behind me.

There was twenty minutes before lunch—enough time to go and change. The girls all had to wear a silly-looking skirt and blouse when they served meals, and I hated that. Give me a pair of baggy shorts and a T-shirt any day.

As I walked to the dorm, where all the girls slept, I felt upset. I had counted on telling Jean-Luc what I had heard. Now I would have to wait—something I'm not very good at. Maybe I would get a chance to talk to him at lunch during a slack time.

But Jean-Luc didn't turn up. At about

12:30 the rush began and the dining room filled up. Fifteen minutes later, he ran in and took over his tables, so there was no time to talk.

Then the Cranks came in and sat down. A black cat must have crossed my path the day they showed up at the lodge a month ago. They had been given a table in the section I looked after.

Nothing was ever good enough for them. The coffee wasn't hot enough, or the toast was too cold, or the eggs were too runny. On and on. And when they weren't nagging at me, they turned on each other.

I picked up the lunch menu and headed over to their table. *Let's get this over with,* I thought. I was worried. Did they know I had overheard them this morning? But when I took their orders they seemed the same as usual.

I came back with two tomato juices and set one down in front of Mr. Crank. And then it happened. As I lifted the second glass, it caught the edge of my tray and tipped. Tomato juice poured over the table and onto Mrs. Crank's lap—right onto her white summer pants.

She jumped to her feet, almost turning the table over, and she started to curse. I didn't know what to do. I grabbed a napkin and tried to mop up some of the juice on her pants. It looked awful—like blood running down her legs.

"Don't touch me!" she shouted and swung her arm back.

Mr. Crank grabbed her arm and said, "C'mon, Sis, let's get out of here!"

Without another word they both left.

She was going to hit me, I thought, as I stood there. She was really going to hit me.

CHAPTER 3

Close to tears, I mopped up the Cranks' table. M. Fontaine came over and talked to me.

"It was just an accident. C'est dommage," he said. "But you're not the first to spill something this summer and you won't be the last. I'll talk to Mrs. Crank and we'll dry clean her pants—or even replace them if we have to. Don't worry about it too much," he told me. He could tell I was upset.

As the last of the diners were leaving, Jean-Luc came over and put his arm around my shoulders. "Are you O.K., Cat?"

he asked, sounding worried.

I looked up and whispered so nobody else could hear, "Jean-Luc, I have to talk to you. Do you have any free time this afternoon?" I asked. I had to tell him about what I had heard in the Cranks' cabin—leaving out the part about my snooping, of course.

"I've got to go back to Knowlton with M. Fontaine for one more load of supplies. We should only be gone for a little over an hour. Maybe I could meet you at the beach as soon as I get back," he finished.

"O.K., I'll meet you there," I said quickly.

"Last one in the water buys patates

frites at the tuck shop," Jean-Luc said, laughing as we left the dining room together.

But I didn't feel like laughing. I had two cabins to clean after lunch, and then I'd be free to meet Jean-Luc. As I worked I thought about all the weird things that had happened this morning. And one of the weirdest had been when Mr. Crank had called Mrs. Crank "Sis." What a funny thing for a husband to call his wife!

I knew the boat tour the Cranks had been talking about. It had to be the one that left the resort at three o'clock. Every day it took the guests on a two-hour trip around the lake, and made a stop at the Brome Lake Duck Farm. Maybe the Cranks would go today—at least they would if Mrs. Crank had her way. I decided to watch if they got on the boat.

I dropped off my keys and supplies, ran to the dorm, and changed into my bathing suit and T-shirt. Outside, I grabbed my towel from the clothesline and headed for the beach.

There was a nice sandy swimming area roped off in front of the main lodge. To the right, where the water was deeper,

there was a dock. That's where rental boats, canoes, and the resort tour boat were tied up.

I laid my towel on the hot sand and plunked down. I could see there were a few people already on the tour boat. And then the Cranks appeared. Mr. Crank looked angry as Mrs. Crank pushed him up the dock to the boat. They didn't look like your average couple out for a fun afternoon. Five minutes later the boat chugged off up the lake, the angry faces of the Cranks growing smaller as it moved away.

I sat on the beach and watched them go with a smile on my face. I must have looked like a real cat that had just swallowed a mouse. Because while I had been waiting, a crazy idea had come into my head. This was a perfect chance to finish looking around in their cabin!

I grabbed my towel and T-shirt and ran up to the office at the back of the main lodge. I peered through the screen door and saw that the office was empty. As I took the key off the pegboard, I stopped. I had to have a reason to go the their cabin again today.

Brainwave! I could clean out their fireplace. Taking the ash pail and scoop from the shed, I went down the dirt road to their cabin.

There was no one around so I quickly let myself in. I stood there for a few seconds, not moving. The curtains were closed to keep out the hot sun, and the only sound was the ticking of a clock.

I began to have second thoughts. Snooping didn't seem like a good idea any more. I had never snooped on purpose before. I just took the chances that came my way. And now I was scared—I just wanted to get out of there as fast as I could.

But if I was seen leaving the cabin with an empty ash pail, it wouldn't look right. I needed to clean the fireplace before I left.

I shoved the metal scoop into the ashes. A cloud of soot and ash floated into the air. This made me cough, and more ashes filled the air. Before I made a bigger mess, I needed a strong draft up the chimney. I reached my arm up the chimney and tried to push the metal damper open all the way. It was stuck and wouldn't move. I could hear something crunching up

there as I pushed.

Trying not to get soot all over my arms, I reached above the damper and felt around. That's when I felt something—something very strange.

My bare knees in the ashes, I reached farther. With a grunt I pulled whatever it was out.

I had found a small, brown metal box. I put it on the floor and tried to lift the lid, but the box was locked. When I shook it, something heavy banged against the sides.

Here was something else for me to figure out. Why had the Cranks hidden a metal box up in the chimney? The Fontaines had a safe in the office where guests could keep anything that was worth a lot.

Then I remembered the key I had found this morning in the dresser—that key just might fit the box!

I got up and brushed off my hands, leaving the box on the floor. In the bedroom I opened the top left-hand drawer of the dresser. Picking up the socks, I unrolled them and took out the key and folded newspaper.

I went back to the main room and tried the key in the box. *It fit!* I turned the key and lifted the lid. My hands were shaking, I was so scared, but what I found inside made me shake even more. Lying in the box was a gun—a very deadly-looking gun. I stared at it, not sure what to do or think.

But I still had the folded newspaper. Quickly I unfolded it. One side had an ad for houses, but the other side was different!

Bank Guard Killed In Robbery, a huge black headline said. It had happened in Montreal the last week in June. Two

armed robbers in ski masks had held up a bank at closing time. The people in the bank, the tellers, and two guards were made to lie on the floor. As the robbers were leaving, a guard tried to pull out his gun and one of the robbers shot him. The second guard went for his gun and they shot him too. The newspaper said one guard was dead and the other one was in hospital. Stocks, bonds, and a large amount of cash had been stolen. A huge police search was under way for the robbers.

I read the clipping a second time, more slowly. There was an awful feeling in the pit of my stomach. All I could do was sit and stare at the headline.

And I guess that's why I didn't hear the door open behind me.

CHAPTER 4

"What the—" said a surprised voice. I spun around to face the door and the newspaper clipping fell to the floor. The Cranks and I stood frozen—staring at each other. *How could they be back here already?* I thought, in a panic.

Mr. Crank swore again. Then he ran over and grabbed me by the arm. "What are you doing here?" he growled.

Before I could say anything, Mrs. Crank grabbed my other arm. She glared at the gun in the open box.

"What's that gun doing here?" she screeched at Mr. Crank. "I told you to

bury the gun outside with the money, you idiot!"

I pulled and tugged, trying to get my arms free. "Let me go! Please, let me go!" I cried.

Mr. Crank clamped his rough hand over my mouth, so I bit him.

"OUCH! Give me a hand with this kid!" he cried out, cupping his hand over my mouth so I couldn't bite him again.

"We've got to keep her quiet," Mrs. Crank said. "Hang on to her while I find something."

She went into the other room. Mr.

Crank stood behind me, one arm tightly around me, his other hand covering my mouth. I struggled, trying to get loose. I tried kicking backward, but it was useless. My bare foot just slid along the floor.

Mrs. Crank came rushing out of the bedroom with a couple of thin belts, a hanky, and a roll of white tape. I knew the tape had come from a first-aid kit in the medicine chest.

I kept trying to get loose, but Mrs. Crank smacked me. "Hold still or I'll give you a punch that will really rattle your brains," she threatened.

She forced the hanky into my mouth, hurting me, then wrapped the tape around my mouth and head. Mr. Crank pulled my arms behind my back and tied my wrists tight with a belt.

"Let's put her in the bathroom. There's no window and nobody will hear any noises she makes," gasped Mrs. Crank.

I was dragged through the bedroom and into the bathroom where they made me step into the tub and kneel down. One of them pushed me down on my stomach. My knees were bent and my feet were up in the air behind me.

While one of them held me down, I felt the other tying my feet together at the ankles. I twisted my head around, trying to see. They both stood there looking down at me, sweating from all the work. "We need another belt. Give me yours," Mrs. Crank ordered.

Mr. Crank took his belt off and handed it to her without a word. Pushing and tugging, she finally got it through the belts that tied my wrists and ankles. I couldn't keep my head up any longer so I lay my cheek down on the bottom of the cool tub.

My wrists and ankles got tugged and yanked about some more before they were done. Then the bathroom door slammed shut and they were gone.

I lay there tied up like a chicken going to market. Tears were rolling down my cheeks and my nose was running. I couldn't open my mouth, and I had a hard time breathing.

I tried hard to calm down by squeezing my eyes shut and taking long slow breaths. My face was all wet and sticky, but at least I could still breathe. Then I twisted my head around again to see behind me.

What an awful fix I was in. The last belt had pulled my ankles and wrists together behind my back. Then it had been wrapped around the bathtub tap. I could hardly move and my arms and legs were starting to ache.

I heard the Cranks' voices out in the bedroom. By lying really still, I could hear what they were saying.

"I *told* you to bury that gun, you brainless idiot!" Mrs. Crank was saying. "What did I do to deserve such a dummy for a brother? You haven't listened to a thing Mom or I have said to you in the last

thirty years. And what made you keep that newspaper clipping!" she hissed.

"You've ruined my plan," she went on. "The cops never would have looked for us in a place like this. We would have been just another stupid couple on vacation. It was a perfect cover."

I could hardly hear what Mr. Crank had to say. He seemed to be having trouble with a comeback.

"If that boat hadn't got engine trouble and turned back, we would never even have found the kid. What made her snoop around here anyway?" she snapped.

"There was nothing but the money to connect us to that robbery. Now we're in big trouble—*thanks to you!*" she hissed. "But there's got to be a way out of this mess."

For the next few minutes only the sound of a dresser drawer slamming shut broke the silence. And then she started up again.

"We'll have to get rid of her and make it look like an accident. She knows too much to let her go."

"But what if she told someone she was coming here?" Mr. Crank asked.

"If anyone shows up asking about her we'll say we haven't seen her," Mrs. Crank answered. "With that guard dying on us, we've had it if they ever catch us. I don't plan on going to jail for the rest of my life," she said. *"No matter what I have to do!"*

CHAPTER 5

I had heard too much. My first panic had turned to horror. *This couldn't be happening to me,* I thought.

In the bedroom the loud voices went on and on. "Here's what we're going to do," Mrs. Crank told her brother. "We need to find out if anyone knows the kid was coming here. I bet the little sneak was looking for something to steal, so she wouldn't tell just anyone where she was going."

My heart sank like a stone in a lake. She was right—no one knew where I was.

"Supper starts in a few minutes," Mrs. Crank said. "I'm going to go, and if anyone asks about you, I'll say you're sick. I'll find out if they're looking for her yet. I don't think they'll start to worry until tonight, and I doubt they'll start looking for her until the morning. By then it'll be too late."

For a second it was very quiet, then Mrs. Crank went on. "Remember those signs posted near the lake below the cabins? You're not supposed to dive there because of rocks. We can make it look like she hit her head and drowned. She's got her bathing suit on so we'll just take her towel down and leave it on the shore," Mrs. Crank said, thinking out loud. "When they find her they'll figure she's just another dumb kid who didn't read the signs."

There was silence. Finally, her brother answered. "But she's just a kid!" he said, sounding upset.

"What else can we do?" she shot back. "It's her—*or us!* We didn't ask her to come snooping around. It's her own fault," she said coldly.

I held my breath, listening through

another long silence.

"O.K.," said Mr. Crank in a shaky voice. "O.K."

I lay there like I was already dead—my body stiff, my mind blank. I shut my eyes tight, as if that would keep away the words I had heard. That's when the bathroom door opened and someone's fingers jabbed me in the side. My eyes flew open.

"She's not going anywhere," Mrs. Crank said, looking down at me. "I'm going to supper and find out what I can. You stay and make sure our snoop doesn't

leave before her last swim." Her awful laugh filled the small room.

"Oh no, you're not!" Mr. Crank said quickly. "You stay with the kid. I'm starved. I didn't get any lunch after you almost hit her, remember?"

Mrs. Crank snapped back at her brother, "Forget it. You got us into this mess, so you're the one who's staying!"

Then I heard her leave the bathroom and slam the cabin door.

Mr. Crank started to curse at his sister. He was really mad. "Who does she think she is," he swore. "This brat couldn't budge if her life depended on it and I'm not going to babysit while Sis sits there stuffing her face." Then he left too, slamming the doors behind him.

The cabin was quiet. Every awful thing that had happened since they caught me came crowding into my mind. I didn't want to believe what was happening. I just wanted to close my eyes, and when I opened them again to be somewhere else—somewhere safe.

I started to cry. *Please God,* I prayed, *just get me out of this, and I'll never snoop again. I promise.*

My nose started dripping again. Then to top it all off, I had to pee. But thinking about that brought me to my senses. I calmed down a little and tried to think.

The Cranks would be gone an hour—maybe longer. The kids would have to cover my tables and that would slow supper down. If I was going to get away, it had to be now.

I started to push and pull against the belts. I was in such a weird position I couldn't get much pressure against them. I tugged and tugged, twisting from side to side, and tried using all my weight on the

belts, but they wouldn't give. After only a few minutes I was beat. My arms and legs were tired and my wrists were sore.

Maybe I *had* stretched or loosened the belts a little, but I wasn't even close to getting my hands or feet loose.

I started to cry again, feeling sorry for myself. I was ready to give up because there was nothing else to do.

I was going to die!

CHAPTER 6

And then I got mad. Mad at myself for getting into this mess. Mad at my parents for letting me come to this stupid resort. Mad at the awful Cranks. I was furious.

I started to jerk my arms and legs around. Like a fish out of water, I flopped and bumped around in the tub, twisting my body like crazy. What did it matter if I broke an ankle or wrist?

At last the belt tied to the tap twisted and I flipped from my stomach onto my right side. Whooosh! A gush of water hit me. Dazed, shocked by the water, I stopped moving. What had happened?

Water was splashing down on me from the shower above. The tap had turned on when the belt attached to it had twisted. It was cold—but at least the tap hadn't turned to the hot water, I thought. I looked back and saw the belt was still wedged around the back of the tap.

I tried to jerk the belt off the tap, but it didn't work. The water kept coming, soaking me through. Now the crazy strength my anger had given me was gone. Both my wrists and ankles had been rubbed raw and were bleeding a little. Blood mixed with the water and flowed down the drain.

It felt like the belts were getting slippery now that they were wet. Did leather stretch or shrink when it got wet? I couldn't remember, but I was going to find out.

Again, I tried to stretch the belts apart. I took turns pushing first my wrists, and then my ankles apart.

Was I going crazy or was there more room between my ankles? I rested a second and then tried again. It hurt so much I wanted to stop, but I was sure now. There *was* more room between my ankles. With each tug and twist, my left foot was coming free.

Another tug and my foot came loose. My left knee slammed hard against the side of the tub. It hurt so much I wanted to cry out or scream.

I lay there, my chest heaving in and out, water splashing around me. Every effort had gone to freeing myself, so I had lost all track of time. My struggles seemed to have gone on forever, but there was no time to rest now.

I shook my right foot free from the belt that had tied my ankles together. My legs and feet were finally free.

I fought to sit back on my heels, my face screwed up from pain, my knees bruised and sore. I stood up unsteadily in the tub. My hands were still tied behind my back and attached to the belt that wrapped around the tap.

Edging to the side of the tub, I stepped carefully onto the floor. The belt tied to the tap was stretched tight so I couldn't go any farther.

I was shaking all over. Water dripped off of me, making small puddles on the floor. My hair hung in tangled strands

over my face. The only reason my teeth weren't chattering was because of the hanky in my mouth. A real cat, soaking wet, couldn't have looked worse.

I shook the hair away from my face and a drop of water fell from my nose. Even though I was standing outside the tub, I was still tied to it.

With one foot against the side, I began pushing against the tub. At the same time I pulled with my arms as hard as I could. Something would have to give. . . .

At last the belt going to the tap broke and I was flung across the room against the bathroom door.

The room spun around me. I staggered across to the toilet and sat down. I put my head down on my knees, and hoped that the dizziness would pass.

Keep going! I told myself. *You can't stop now!*

Every part of me ached as I got up and crossed to the bathroom door. Even with my wrists tied together, I could still move my fingers and grab the doorknob.

Then I had my first real piece of luck. This door only locked from the inside. So after a few clumsy tries, I managed to turn the knob and push open the door. After everything else I had done, this was a cinch.

I stumbled through the bedroom, into the main room, and over to the cabin door. But my luck had run out.

The door was locked!

CHAPTER 7

I leaned against the locked front door, my head resting on the smooth wood. *There's no end to this nightmare,* I thought, as a few new tears rolled down my cheeks. Getting out of that bathroom had seemed impossible, but I *had* done it and I couldn't give up now!

How long ago had the Cranks gone to dinner? I wondered. I knew there was a clock on the cabin wall so I limped over and stared at it. I could hardly believe that dinner had started just a half hour ago. It felt like hours had gone by since Mr. Crank had stormed out of the cabin.

What if they came back and found me now? Panic twisted my insides. I wanted to scream and throw myself against the front door. I had to get out right away.

The only other way out was to go through a window or get some help. Hands still tied behind me, I pushed my head around the curtains, and looked out. No one was around to help.

I drew back and looked carefully at the windows in the cabin. The easiest one to get out of was in the wall opposite the front door, and looked out over the lake. It was a good-sized picture window with no screen. Turning around, I grabbed the curtain and pulled it aside with short jerks. Then I dragged a small chair under the window and climbed up onto it. But when I was about to jump through, I stopped. I could see myself lying on the ground, cut by big pieces of broken glass. I knew I would have to break the window first. Another problem, I thought, almost in tears. It would be hard to break the glass with my hands tied behind me. It would be easier to kick it out, but I was in my bathing suit and my feet were bare.

Then I had the answer to my problem.

I remembered a pair of slippers I had seen in the bedroom this morning. They would protect my feet. My legs almost gave way as I jumped down from the chair and staggered to the bedroom. Sure enough, there were the slippers near the bed. I pushed my feet into them and clumped back out.

  Getting back up on the chair with the slippers on wasn't easy. Then I had to balance on one foot as I tapped the other against the window glass. Nothing happened. I tapped harder but the glass still wouldn't break. I was afraid my leg

would be cut if my foot went through the glass.

Come on, Cat, you've got to do better than that, I said to myself. Pulling my foot way back, I smacked it hard against the window.

Crraack! Glass broke and fell everywhere. For a heart-stopping second, I swayed, and almost fell on the jagged glass left in the window.

There were still large pieces left in the frame so I kicked them out with my foot. At last, the hole was big enough for me to get through.

All this while, a voice inside of me kept saying, *Hurry up! Hurry up!* There was no time to do any more.

I put one foot on the window sill and looked outside. Most of the glass had fallen straight out from the window to the ground about a metre down. I would have to jump away to one side.

Go! Go! I said to myself. I put my other foot on the sill and jumped.

CHAPTER 8

WHOOMPH! I landed heavily on my right side. I tumbled and rolled down a small slope, and stopped with a sudden thud. A tree had got in my way. I lay there dazed, out of breath, my face partly buried in the dirt.

Painfully, I rolled over onto my side. I snorted dirt and pine needles out of my nose. Up above me, between some branches, was a clear blue sky.

When I sat up, it was impossible to tell what part of me hurt the most. My legs and feet were stinging. I could see thin trickles of blood oozing out of all the cuts

below my knees.

    Struggling to my feet, I walked like a drunk around to the other side of the cabin. The slippers had fallen off when I jumped, and the bottoms of my feet were cut. I had to walk on the outside edges of them. Step by aching step, I climbed the small path that led up from the cabin to the dirt road. Turning right, I limped toward the main lodge.

    I hobbled slowly down the road with my head down. Suddenly I stopped. Somewhere ahead of me, around a bend in the road, I could hear voices. As I stood there, the voices were getting louder—coming toward me.

A stab of fear shot through me. Were the Cranks coming back? The voices were still too far away for me to know. I looked around, but there wasn't a single person in sight to help me. I couldn't let them find me here on the road, *alone!*

I moved as quick as I could toward some trees and bushes. Then I threw myself under a bush and wiggled farther in, trying to hide.

As I hid in the bushes breathing hard, the voices came closer. Soon they were

passing by where I lay.

But both the voices were female and they were speaking French—*it wasn't the Cranks!*

Help at last, I thought. I tried to get up, but the thick branches of the bush pushed down on me. I squirmed forward, got my feet under me, and stood up.

But the women were gone. I couldn't believe they hadn't heard me rustling in the bushes. If they had, they must have figured I was a chipmunk or something.

I stood there shaking—not able to call out because of my gag. For the first time I thought about where I was going. So far all I had wanted to do was get far away from that cabin. Now I needed people—and not just anyone. I wanted to get to Jean-Luc and the Fontaines.

I headed for the main lodge, ready to dive into some bushes again if I had to. Jean-Luc and the Fontaines should be in the dining room or the kitchen. Even the thought of the Cranks being there didn't slow me down. They wouldn't be able to touch me with all those people around.

I saw no one in the five long minutes it took me to get to the back of the main lodge.

At last I stumbled around to the side of the lodge, and climbed the wooden steps to the door. I stood in front of the screen door to the dining room.

Peering through the screen, I could see that the dining room was full. The clink of dishes and the smell of spaghetti, my favourite, drifted out to me. My stomach growled.

A couple were leaving, coming toward me. I couldn't open the door myself, so I stood to one side and I waited—nervous, keyed up.

As the door swung open, I pushed forward, tripped over the doorway, and fell flat on the dining-room floor.

I had made it.

CHAPTER 9

I lay on the floor for a second, too tired to get up, but the noise in the dining room continued. Hadn't anybody noticed me?

I struggled to get up one more time. Halfway to my feet, I felt someone helping me. It was Jean-Luc.

"C'est toi, Cat?" he asked in a strange voice.

I could imagine how awful I must have looked. My whole body was covered with dust and dirt and scratches, and dried blood made little patterns on my legs. I was a mess with my tangled hair, taped mouth, and tied hands.

    I flung myself at Jean-Luc, almost knocking both of us to the floor. His arms tightened around me, holding me up.

    Now the whole room was silent. I saw everyone looking at me—surprised, shocked, or puzzled, the faces stared at me.

    Except for the Cranks!

    They were at their table whispering to each other. They knew who I was, and what had happened.

    "Are you O.K., Cat? What's going on?" Jean-Luc asked. "I was worried when you didn't show up at the beach."

    Of course I couldn't answer with the tape

on my mouth. But now, with Jean-Luc beside me and all these people around, I didn't feel afraid.

And when I saw the Cranks getting ready to leave, I got angry.

Pulling away from Jean-Luc, I marched to where the Cranks sat. Then very calmly, I kicked Mrs. Crank in the leg. She jumped back, knocking over her chair.

Jean-Luc and now M. Fontaine were beside me at the table saying, "What's going on? What's happened to you, Cat?"

"This kid's crazy!" Mrs. Crank cried out. "She needs her head examined." She gave me a little push and started to walk quickly toward the door with her brother following after her.

I wasn't letting these two get away that easily, not after all they had done to me.

As fast as I could, I made it over to the doorway. As Mrs. Crank was pulling the screen door open I pushed against her arm. She let go, surprised, and the door smacked shut. Then I put my body between her and the door.

"Get out of my way," she snarled, grabbing my arm as her brother grabbed my other arm.

But Jean-Luc and M. Fontaine had followed me over to the door. "Let her go!" Jean-Luc shouted.

"Excusez," M. Fontaine joined in. "Mr. and Mrs. Crank, please wait until we can get this girl's gag off. Then she can explain what's happened to her, and why she doesn't want you to go."

"Quick, the other door!" Mr. Crank hissed to Mrs. Crank. Then they both took off, running, and I started to limp after them.

The only other door in the dining room was a swinging one that went to the kitchen. Just before the Cranks got to it, they ran right into a group of people standing near it. One man was knocked into a table that turned over. Dishes, glasses, and food went crashing to the floor.

Someone was screaming—lots of people were yelling and shouting. It was crazy.

I was halfway across the room when Jean-Luc and M. Fontaine dashed past me. The Cranks had pushed past the rest of the people and ran through the swinging door. Jean-Luc and M. Fontaine went after them.

Then I made it to the door. I pushed it open with my hip and edged around it into the kitchen. I was just in time to see something I would remember for the rest of my life.

The centre of the kitchen is filled with a big work area. It has huge stoves and counters where dishes are stacked. Mr. Crank was running up one side, and Mrs. Crank up the other, toward a back door.

Before Mrs. Crank could reach the door, Jean-Luc took a flying leap and tackled her. She cried out and down they went, sliding along the tile floor together. Finally, Jean-Luc sat on her, pinning her down.

Mr. Crank turned to look at his sister when she called out. He ran smack into a bus boy who was carrying a tubful of dirty dishes. Mr. Crank, the bus boy, and the tub of dishes crashed to the floor. Plates, glasses, and cups bounced and smashed on the hard tile.

A stunned silence came over the kitchen. All you could hear was Mrs. Crank cursing and Mr. Crank wheezing, trying to catch his breath.

M. Fontaine took charge. He picked up a frying pan and went over to where Mr. Crank lay on the floor. He stood over him, almost daring him to get up.

Then he turned to Mme. Fontaine, who had been in the kitchen when our weird chase took us there. "Claudette, please help Cathy. Maybe she can tell us what in the world is going on here!"

Mme. Fontaine came over to me and looked me up and down from head to toe. "C'est terrible," she said, shaking her head.

Carefully she pulled the end of the tape loose, unwound it from my head, and pulled the hanky from my mouth.

I gave a big gasp and started to choke.

Snatching in great gulps of air, I coughed and coughed. "They were going to kill me!" I said, still choking. "They were going to kill me!"

CHAPTER 10

Mme. Fontaine cut my hands free and took me to her office. I sat there, shivering, as she called the police. Then Mme. Fontaine asked me a lot of questions, and in a shaky voice I told my story. I didn't leave out a thing, not even about my snooping. As I told her, I kept wondering what she was thinking—and what Jean-Luc and the others would think.

It didn't take long for the police to get there. I watched from a small window as the Cranks were handcuffed and put in a police car.

I couldn't believe it was over. But mixed in with my relief, I felt ashamed. Everyone was going to find out about me snooping around in the cabins.

Then the door opened and M. Fontaine walked in with Jean-Luc right behind him. My heart flip-flopped.

As soon as Jean-Luc saw me, he came over. He crouched down beside my chair. "Are you O.K., Cat?" he asked me.

"I'm O.K. now," I said. I had to fight not to burst into tears, but not because I was sad. There was something special about the way Jean-Luc smiled at me—

something that said, *It's all right, Cat.*

M. Fontaine spoke up from where he was sitting on the corner of Mme. Fontaine's desk. "Well, Cathy," he said, "I'd better get you to the hospital in Sherbrooke. You might have some pieces of glass still in your legs, and once the shock wears off, you're going to be very worn out. By tomorrow you won't be able to move," he said with a little laugh.

"I can barely move now," I told him, trying to smile.

M. Fontaine went on, "They may want to keep you overnight at the hospital. The police are going to meet us there to get a statement from you—if you feel ready for that."

Mme. Fontaine broke in. "Well, Cathy—I think you've used up a few of your nine lives with this adventure. I have to call your parents and let them know what's happened. I think they'll be down to see you and maybe to take you home," she said.

But I had some ideas of my own. If only I could get the Fontaines on my side. "I was hoping that you and M. Fontaine would let me stay for the rest of the summer," I broke in. "I wouldn't blame you if you didn't trust me," I added in a hurry. "I know I don't deserve that. Everyone at the resort is going to know about my snooping. But I want to stick it out—if you're willing to take the chance."

"It depends on what your parents have to say about that," Mme. Fontaine replied. "I'll talk it over with them and see how they feel. But remember, it's not going to be easy for you after the whole story comes out."

"I know," I told her.

"As far as trusting you," she went on, "I have a feeling you've learned something important. I don't think we're going to have to worry about that." Then she added with a short cough, "And maybe, par chance, all of us have done *some* kind of snooping."

M. Fontaine stood up and said, "Well, I think I had better get this young lady to the hospital. She needs to see a doctor."

Jean-Luc took my hand and helped pull me to my feet. "I'd like to go with Cat to the hospital," he told the others.

"Good idea," M. Fontaine said, going out the door.

Not letting go of my hand, Jean-Luc turned to follow M. Fontaine. But then I stopped Jean-Luc, and, hating to do it, pulled my hand free.

   I just couldn't wait any more. Blushing, I asked them to wait and went straight for the washroom.

About the Author

Prem Omkaro lives in the country near the village of Killaloe, Ontario. She has been a Jill of all trades over the years and currently works in a commercial greenhouse. This, her first book, was inspired by her son David who said one day, "Don't you ever feel like doing something really different?"

How many **Series Canada** titles have you read?

by Paul Kropp

Hot Cars
Run Away
No Way
Dirt Bike
Snow Ghost
Wild One
Spin Out
Amy's Wish
Get Lost
Tough Stuff

Dope Deal
Burn Out
Dead On
Fair Play
Gang War
Baby, Baby
Micro Man
Take Off
Head Lock
Split Up

by William Bell

Metal Head

by Martyn Godfrey

Fire! Fire!
Rebel Yell
Break Out

Ice Hawk
Wild Night
The Beast

by John Ibbitson

The Wimp

by Sylvia McNicoll

Jump Start

If you enjoyed this book,
you may also enjoy reading . . .

DEAD ON
What is making the strange noises in the hall outside Larry's room? It can't be a ghost. Larry doesn't believe in ghosts. But someone—or something— keeps leading him to the attic of the old house.

DOPE DEAL
Brian has to face a lot of problems. He gets busted by the cops, has to move back home, and beats up his own brother. But his biggest problem comes when he takes on a whole motorcycle gang.

GANG WAR
Jack and the Punks think they're tough. But Charlie and his friends don't like getting pushed around. The two gangs fight it out in one last rumble.

TOUGH STUFF
Nikki was always tough—even after the judge made her do volunteer work at the hospital. Nikki wasn't going to let that change her. She'd show Jake and the gang just how tough she really was.

REBEL YELL
SC already has enough trouble with school and the Hell Cats. Then Willy Boy comes to school with a gun and SC has to try to stop a killing. But . . . can he?

RUNAWAY

Kathy wishes she were a goldfish. She has some good reasons—her father gets drunk and beats her, her best friend drives her crazy, and her boyfriend wants to get too friendly. Will she be better off if she runs away?

SPIN OUT

Marc was just taking his '57 Chevy for a spin. When he saw the flashing light, he thought it meant another ticket. But that flashing light was the start of a night full of adventure.

THE BEAST

Kelly just wants some time by herself out in the bush. She didn't think that Rodger would show up. But she was glad to have him with her when she had to face The Beast . . . .

WILD ONE

Kate saves Wild One from Banner's whip and gets to train the horse herself. But that's only a start. Can she prove he can race before it's too late?

Have you heard of **Series 2000?**

by Paul Kropp

Jo's Search
Not Only Me
Baby Blues
The Victim Was Me

Death Ride
Under Cover
We Both Have Scars

by Martyn Godfrey

The Last War
More Than Weird
In the Time of the Monsters

by John Ibbitson

The Wimp and the Jock
The Wimp and Easy Money
Starcrosser
The Big Story

by Marilyn Halvorson

Bull Rider

by William Bell

Death Wind

by Lesley Choyce

Hungry Lizards
Some Kind of Hero

by Dayle Gaetz

Spoiled Rotten

by Jennifer McVaugh

Hello, Hello;

Note: Teacher's Guides for both **Series Canada** and **Series 2000** are also available.

For more information, write:
Maxwell Macmillan Canada
1200 Eglinton Ave. East, Suite 200
Don Mills, Ontario M3C 3N1
or call: **(416) 449-6030**

DANGER FLOWER

JACLYN DESFORGES

DANGER FLOWER

poems

Copyright © 2021 Jaclyn Desforges

All rights reserved

Palimpsest Press
1171 Eastlawn Ave.
Windsor, Ontario. N8S 3J1
www.palimpsestpress.ca

Book and cover design by Kate Hargreaves (CorusKate Design)
Author photograph by Jesse Valvasori
Edited by Jim Johnstone

 Anstruther Books

Palimpsest Press would like to thank the Canada Council for the Arts, and the Ontario Arts Council for their support of our publishing program. We also acknowledge the assistance of the Government of Ontario through the Ontario Book Publishing Tax Credit.

 Canada Council for the Arts / Conseil des Arts du Canada    ONTARIO ARTS COUNCIL / CONSEIL DES ARTS DE L'ONTARIO   Ontario — Ontario Media Development Corporation

Library and Archives Canada Cataloguing in Publication

Title: Danger flower / Jaclyn Desforges.
Names: Desforges, Jaclyn, 1988- author.
Description: Poems.
Identifiers: Canadiana (print) 20210266449 | Canadiana (ebook) 20210266473 | ISBN 9781989287835 (softcover) | ISBN 9781989287897 (EPUB) | ISBN 9781989287910 (PDF)
Classification: LCC PS8607.E75815 D36 2021 | DDC C811/.6—dc23

PRINTED AND BOUND IN CANADA

CONTENTS

ROSARY PEA

Reverse-Maid	11
Enlightened Witness	12
At Five I Understood Everything	13
Father Figure	14
Crabapples	16
#Blessed	17
Party Girl	18
Pony Closet	19
Wetland	20
There's Very Little Here That's Necessary	21
Home Address	22
Homecoming	23
Nesting Dolls	24

BABY'S BREATH

A Process Of Maturation	27
Birth	29
Episodic Depression	30
Ventilation	31
Climate Apocalypse Parenting Tips	32
Opossum Poem	33
Things Fade	34
Novel Therapies	35

WOLF'S BANE

Forest Fire	39
15c After A Polar Vortex	40
I'd Rather Be Drab	41
Hello Nice Man	42
An Incel Steps On A Snail	43
Secret Doorway	45
Survival Strategies	46
Pics Or It Didn't Happen	47
Pillow Talk	49
Danger Flower	50
The End	51

LAZARUS BELL

Tiger Garden	55
Reality	56
Sourdough	57
Nerve Signals	58
Thirsty	59
I Dropped Them All	60
Freeze	61
I'd Say Things Are Now Sufficiently Absurd	62
Trauma Panorama	63
It's The Small Things That Save Us	66
Acknowledgements	67
About the Author	69

ROSARY PEA

REVERSE-MAID

The winter-est light is the light of this cathedral
It's blue-ish, holy as my fingernails

We listen to the baptism
All nine pounds of her wailing in the water
All nine pounds of her slipping through the bishop's hands

Out of reach of her father
Out of reach of her mother

So Jesus himself steps down from the window
And lifts her from the water by one small foot

We look at her head, which is the head of a fish now
And her body, still kicking, still a human girl's

She's the largest perch ever caught in the county
They hang a photograph of Jesus at the Bait & Tackle

ENLIGHTENED WITNESS

I'm afraid of nothing
except doing the wrong thing.
I'm afraid of that every second.

Somewhere, a faucet's dripping.
Somewhere, my indiscretions
are hooking up in a broom closet.

Meanwhile, I've packed my ears with nettles.
Meanwhile, I've lost how it feels to be found.

I'm still here, but he can't see me.
If a man shouts in the forest and there's no one to hear,
who will help him process his emotions?

AT FIVE I UNDERSTOOD EVERYTHING

There are pussy willows growing
outside of certain women's houses.

There are bodies inside of bodies
inside of bodies inside of houses.

There are seeds inside of summer
inside of winter inside of houses.

There's a lawn inside me.
Uncertainty.

Nobody can see
behind my eyelids but me.

FATHER FIGURE

One day you'll tell my mother
at least my kids are consistent.

Yours goes goodgoodgoodgood   bad

But I'm not bad yet.

Flat on my back in some lake.
Someone brought a hot plate.

I make friends with a seagull.
My Tamagotchi gets sand inside,
never turns on again.

Zebra mussels cut me & I wade to shore,
dripping like murder

and you glance at me
like you're afraid.
Well, maybe you should be.

I think there's a place where two people
can speak to each other from a distance,

some campground bonfire
where foreheads glow gold.

When you can't see clearly—
when you're eight, or forty,

with a mortgage, a life—

I know it can all seem murky.
Impossible.

I know a child can rise bloodstriped
from a body of water

and you can look past her
to the horizon,
see nothing at all.

CRABAPPLES

She tells herself it's okay to want something,
runs her nail along a pinecone.

A hundred wooden tongues. A vortex.

A severed arm shoots out of the earth.
It opens its palm: a plump Macintosh.
There are no more apple trees,

only cuttings, thin branches
wrapped in wire, propped up
by metal stakes.

She doesn't pick her own,
buys a plastic bag instead.
No use pretending.

She cores apples by hand,
drops them in the pot unpeeled.
They bubble up on low.

Later, she'll classify the result as sauce,

she'll stir away the lumps,
sting her cuticles with lemon juice,
wooden spoon it into jars.

She'll kiss her reflection in the mirror,
leave the lipstick mark for days.

#BLESSED

Sunbeams aren't something I notice.
Mostly it's my own breasts, bobbing with effort
like I'm a man writing the story of a woman
and the way her nipples strain politely

against the confines of her blouse.
I think I'm neat. I think I'm good enough.
Still, a cell memory of strangulation
tickles the pale of my throat, my author squeezing,

waiting for irises to bloom in recognition:
today is the last day &

my lips curl in gratitude to have occupied
the others in this rent-to-own body,
all those low voices cradling me in private, in public,
making me feel safe when I wasn't.

PARTY GIRL

Can't stop seeing cockroaches
and I've never had a cockroach.

Want to tell you—I had a ball gown.
Want to tell you—someone threw the bouquet.

I think it was me. In my dreams no one RSVPs
to my wedding, the snow-white sheet
where I lay my belongings for inspection.
Empty jam jars, Tupperware, handkerchiefs

no one's sneezed in. I'd invite you inside
but there's nothing of note. Just the oak
that poisons me and feeds the deer.

Still, I'll leave the door open. Come in,
don't wipe your feet.

I'm wild and available,
making a mess of the floor.

And the roots, the cuttings,
they never take—
not in soil, not in water.

PONY CLOSET

All the guests are here and also fruitcake
Which arrived alone in a minivan

The potpourri has been refreshed
Ice cream is melting on the front steps

Everyone's feet are sticky
Everyone's fingernails are picking at apple skins

The games we play help prepare us for the future
When I slip into the closet to play with plastic

Horses nobody notices I like the smell of dust
On carpet today is my day

My pony closet quiet day I'm so lucky

God's looking at me straight today yesterday
Was my brother's day and the sky filled up with lightning

At least the lawn has that green smell now
So the worms are happy here

WETLAND

If you wanted me, you'd take me.
Here, by the cattails—

I'm perched in the long grass
like an open drawer.

Dense strands of purple
loosestrife. The matted roots
swallow everything.

Would it matter if I told you
I was waiting?

No. You'd call me home.

You only want to know me halfway.
Push my bangs aside.
Shut the door.

THERE'S VERY LITTLE HERE THAT'S NECESSARY

I climbed a rope nobody yelled for.
I slid down someone else's pole.

What's essential is hydration.

What's essential is the way he looks
across a still body of water,
the way he counts the trees.

Can you swim that far, I ask him,
taunting the man who measures me back,
the man who finds me wanting
and small.

HOME ADDRESS

I know you, he says, and he's wrong.

Somewhere inside her there is a forest
and in the forest there is a meadow
and in the meadow there is a cottage

and in the cottage she's peeling potatoes
and boiling water for soup.

Confident of her whereabouts in a way
only a man could be confident—

he's two towns over at the abandoned church
pounding on the door.

HOMECOMING

The sapphire wedding ring that gives me a rash,
a watercolour painting in a dollar store frame,
a printer out of ink. An outdoor table
we never assembled in a heavy brown box
against the window

      and through the glass maple trees
that don't know their own names and scaffolding.

      I don't notice I'm too busy

skinny dipping for you in my memory's
Mill Pond. This is what you wanted, right?
Boys in dress shirts under football uniforms.
Girls bracketed by tanning booths.
Truckers honking at me in my winter coat

and my boyfriend sweeping up pigeon shit
for thirteen dollars an hour.

We melted together in a pot of casual whiteness,
bought our two-fours of Coors Light every payday,
walked clear across town after the streetlights fired up
to Amanda Stevenson's house party.

Good to be home.
There were Pixy Stix on the front porch
with that sister who never calls.
There were monogamous swans, probably.

NESTING DOLLS

Sometimes I feel imbued with a coral colour, an earth pink, like it's coming out my elbows. Sometimes I feel like my whole body's a remembering, and the part of me that's riding a scooter, *scooting to school*, is hanging out with Emma Williamson's remembering, and inside every one of those rememberings there's a hard kernel. So if we all dissolved at the same time— if we got together for a middle school reunion and lined up for a beer and then melted—what remained would be a series of pebbles. Somebody who saw it later would know nothing about us. When I think about what comes after, what comes later in the sequence, I get nervous. I start to think maybe I really am here for nothing. I start to think about her trampoline—Emma's—and pressing my back against the elastic. About the orange allness even when my eyes were squeezed shut.

BABY'S BREATH

A PROCESS OF MATURATION

Here is Anna and here
is Anna's body and here
is Anna's hat and here

are Anna's softish hands and here
is a bucket of unfiltered milk and here
is a sprig of girlhood lavender and here
is a pot of pine-needle tea and here

is somebody else's baby and here
is a mewling basket of cats and here
is a musical with multiple leads and here
is a bucket of everyone's shit and here

is a trickle of blackberry jam and here
is a melodic humming and purr and here
is a predestined uterine tug and here
is a trampoline with no safety features and here

is a face pressed hard to brick wall and here
is a body that fattens and bounces and here
is astral projection and song and here
is a register nobody hears and here

is a man
with morally neutral features

who will solve Anna's consciousness problem
the latent wondering *why am I still here*

the mammalian power to replicate
and the thought undertow: she's a passageway

for the entrance of progeny
she arches her back and beneath her body they scurry
transform her from protagonist to door
and when she dies

she hopes tigers will eat her

BIRTH

Perfection is bleeding an average amount overnight
Perfection rolls my eyes backward until the horizon flips

I like the paper dresses and how the hallways smell clean
If I were a sturgeon I'd live forever, wriggle in the mud
And lay eggs and wash my face with cold water

I don't move but there are wishes inside me
And a catheter and what drips out is ordinary blood

My dreams aren't dreams that come from soft places
If I sleep I'm afraid I'll forget her

EPISODIC DEPRESSION

There is a cul de sac
There is a tangle of fishing line in an oak tree

The cicadas leave their skins behind
They won't stop crying

The room inside of me is empty
I'm not here anymore there's been a murder

Nature is as unknowable as a cumulus cloud
That ice cream truck's been circling the block for days

When I get back I'll give myself a scolding
And a rat to care for with a long soft tail

Their father is here but this isn't his house
Everything's gridlike, he can't move diagonally

My daughter's apron is covered in flour
All she does is cry and knead

VENTILATION

When you make fire you have to keep making fire
Or everything will get damp

One day your mother won't save you

One day you'll be alone with all your babies
And no cheques in the mail

You'll cook chicken legs like your mother did
You'll be afraid like your mother was

One day there'll be no one in your kitchen but you

Nothing left but a ceiling fan
Nothing left but damp feet under a ceiling fan

Your children will come inside and you'll feed them
You'll only hurt them in ways you can't possibly control

You'll hyperventilate but only when the sun's up
At night the sky's so black you feel swallowed and happy

Especially with your seatbelt on tight
Especially with the car drifting

An inbreath is every mother's favourite sound

But your mother's not here
So the moon follows you home

CLIMATE APOCALYPSE PARENTING TIPS

An animal eats another animal with a knife
and fork. My daughter asks

>   will I die really
>   really when I am really old

and I smear butter on a roll. I say

>   yes
>   you will die and me
>   and your father and your grandmother
>   and your friends and your children in their cold
>
>   dark dens; every nest of squirrelish
>   babies will dry up in the sun.

She swallows.
We drive to the fair

where the sky is the colour of deep-fried
chocolate. I shove a fistful
of tickets in the Ferris wheel man's hand.

He leans against the lever.

Up and up, our sandals
dangling. All her grown-up teeth.
I pull the bar down.

OPOSSUM POEM

At midnight, I flick the porch-
light and catch an opossum
in the flood, three babies
clinging to her back, moon-
eyed. At birth, they're small
as honeybees. Thirteen
to a teaspoon beginning
their odyssey from the mainland
of belly to pouch. But this
isn't a story about an opossum,
or about seeing that opossum
spooked in my apple tree,
or about peering over glass
fragments pricking the soles
of my feet. It's not about
my daughter staring up
from my breast, gulping,
or the thousand ways I've seen
her die in the years
she's been alive. It's the rest
of it—the biannual scrubbing
of the outdoor windows,
that porch at dusk with dry
Riesling in a chilled glass,
listening to cicadas
with a hand on my knee,
watching her string up paper
flowers and feeling
the graze of light sunburn.

THINGS FADE

1.

Diminuendos, acne scars, haircuts.
I buy a lightbulb-studded mask that makes me look like a stormtrooper.
It's supposed to clear my skin. Instead it blinds me –

twenty-one tiny eclipses
and I stare directly at them all.

2.

Men don't look at me anymore.

I blame this on my baby, my pixie cut, the fine lines
on my forehead. Another part wonders —

can they tell it's a lost cause? Above every woman's crown,
the odds float there like a halo.

3.

Late October. The sun sets early.
I light scented candles
just to snuff them out again.

NOVEL THERAPIES

When you get mastitis they tell you to lie
down. So I carve two openings

in the Earth and lean forward. I set
my chin in the mud. Insects come
with their tongues.

It's better than nursing. *Your nipples
actually taste sweet,* some childless lover
said once. She made me wash

her dishes. What's that sensation—
they've probably banned it in France—
like restless leg syndrome,

that fundamental incongruence
between outer action
and inner impulse,

between *ice the cupcakes*
and *lie down dead*

between outside and inside
when outside is buttercream

and inside—
well, the inside
is multiplying.

WOLF'S BANE

FOREST FIRE

Slut makes me think of the Grand Canyon
Slut makes me think of a door

Slut makes me think of those clouds—stop-motion
When I cut through the forest to school

When ink goes inside you, does it ever come out?
Boys behind oak trees yell *Slut*

When you open the door you're in a bathtub
So you take off all your clothes

I liked it better when I thought the trees were talking

Say slut three times and I appear
Say slut four times and I get a master's degree

Slut makes me think of the forest floor

15C AFTER A POLAR VORTEX

Sex raises its head from a death's worth of winter.

I don't need to do anything, just order this tea,
just stand all thick and breathing in this line.

Do you see? It's not about me.
I didn't ask for this.

We're all answering some call, some fragrance.

I'D RATHER BE DRAB

Beautiful moths do not have mouths.
Without mouths, they cannot eat.

Take the cecropia moth.
Lacking functional mouthparts
or a working digestive system,

she can only mate,

releasing perfume to attract a male
from seven miles away.

After, she'll lay a hundred eggs
that hatch into tiny black caterpillars

which, having mouths,
will feed on maple, birch and apple
before spinning their autumn cocoons.

Once they emerge, cecropia live no more
than two weeks, their bodies often
preserved for viewing in entomological frames.

Common moths feast on wedding gowns
and their bodies are kept by no one.

HELLO NICE MAN

You don't believe in violence
against women, against me.

You don't believe in abandonment
until you abandon me.

Somewhere a child's learning
not to cough around you.

Somewhere giant hogweed
is going to seed.

It's mystical, really. Old Testament God
with morning wood which means nothing;

some small sharp thing
in the folds of his bathrobe.

AN INCEL STEPS ON A SNAIL

The world flows inside my shell
and out again. You think I'm afraid
but I like the dark. I have no ears.

You like to imagine me retracted,
every impulse curtailed, divine justice,
something punished.

But nothing stalks me. Only you,
your dirty sneakers. You resent
the slippery hollow of my making.

Love, I'm sorry you don't carry
your home on your back—

there are no pink tongues to taste you.
No slick membranes to plumb
but your own.

Would you like to crush me? You can't.
The only suffering in this forest is yours.
I appear and recede with your moon,

I like the way you feel, hovering over me,
and the sun and the soil like you too, and the wind,
it likes the way your face is set.

Open and closed at once,
an appeal, a spectre.

You think you were made for nothing, exempt
from this wildness, a wilted mistake of your cruel
imagined Nature. But don't despair.

One of my sisters will save you—
slip inside the coiled mouth of your ear,
nibble a hollow, let the light in.

SECRET DOORWAY

Surprise! I'm here to tell you I escaped
through a sewer line, in a blue prairie frock
on dishwashed hands and knobby knees.
I travelled north and north and north

through that subterranean tube, all the while forgetting
what they taught me about dinosaur riding, about Tater Tots,
about front hugs, about God. All the while collecting
opinions like Dollar Store gemstones, new and sparkly,

but hard to brag about. My perm unfurled
four miles in and I ripped off my shit-soaked dress
after five. When I emerged from that manhole,
I pulled my hair into a slapdash bun

and wandered the wheat fields of Saskatchewan.
I found myself a Tim Hortons, a cup of devil's brew,
double-double, which I sipped buck naked
as the Canadians politely looked elsewhere.

SURVIVAL STRATEGIES

Before we knew what extinction meant,
we put on a one-woman show.

Gwenevere was the mouth.
Moody Judy kept blushing; she played
the dimpled thigh.

Forty women propped us upright,
though we never learned their names.

At intermission we mingled,
mocked manspreaders, drank white
and weren't beauty standards unacceptable?
Weren't mirrors something to break?

In the end, we fled to the woods.
In the end, Susan stopped epilating her lip

though Paul with the pretty okay sales job
declared her a goddess anyway.

We high-fived over how little this mattered
to our glittering tiger-striped selves,
drank kombucha we totally wanted. Though

some of us fucked Paul anyway, behind
the last redwood tree, soft-faced against the bark
as he moaned *baby, you feel perfect.*

PICS OR IT DIDN'T HAPPEN

When you have tits and the internet
you will eventually put your tits on the internet.

I offer myself at the altar
and write *these are my tits, on the internet (F30)*

in which (F30) identifies myself
to men with eyes on the internet

which is really just a space/time continuum of tits
which is really just a crystalline lattice of tits

and men write *does it turn you on
when I fap to your tits on the internet?*

And men write *look what happened to my cock
when I looked at your tits on the internet*

and I write *yes* and I write *I see*
because I do, really, I really do see

that somewhere, now, there are bears, fucking
and somewhere salmon are swimming upstream

and bacteria are getting it on
and there's a wide wide Earth full of wanting.

Because to stand unhurried at the precipice of desire,
to stand naked at the door, unafraid

to stare back—
is a thing for me.

PILLOW TALK

A cold dry rock in space is dead until we terraform it. It's like the justice system but backwards, the object consecrated in the act of enveloping. It's a welcoming. A rumination similar to, but different from, an altar. Take note of mammals with their mouths full of grass. Of our bodies' ineffectual edges. When you're inside me, you are me. Are you alarmed by spray? Sex is water, the molecular suture of life, the only flowable gift in space. We act like it's some kind of power. It's no more a power than the power to swallow—a biological act of selective absorption, the nighttime pursuit of nutrients. Sin is cold death and we wash it away. Then, in the fields, the lambs come.

DANGER FLOWER

Feeling musical this morning, like a Venus flytrap,
some prickly-cunted girl you weren't expecting.

Takes a lot to snap me shut now, to take concrete steps toward
    meat.

You get confident, you know? A backless number,
shadowed face pics, un-photoshopped tattoos.
You forget what it feels like to be prey.

I say *you*, but of course I mean *me*. Some bickering collective,
every version of myself locked in a greenhouse.

The fourteen year old keeps her head up,
likes padded bras and Bonne Bell and kissing boys
    who smoke.

Here she tries on body like glitter gloss and fishnets.
Here she's super psyched for champagne flutes.

Me. What even is that? Just a stretch of trembling smiles.
They say *you're not invincible,* but what if I am?
What if I'm exactly as safe as I think?

THE END

My poems are eggshells made of the eggshells of other eggshells
and birdhouses made from bones

I don't like weighing myself anymore not after last time

My eyelashes keep falling in my soup
A sturgeon appears in silhouette on the moon

This is the life I want to live
I keep the window open I'm not scared of bees

I think a baby might fix me
I guess what I'm wondering is how we keep breathing

If there have always been bodies in the streets
Today maybe I'll just be direct

It won't be a fairy tale
I won't make it to the end of whatever this is

LAZARUS BELL

TIGER GARDEN

There is no cacophony outside,
only inside, only pollen
and ventricles like a simulation

and outside still the buildings are standing
plightless and slow, all the women

in mourning. It is small and green,
easily snapped by a rabbit,
and inside the stem is her body

and nightgowned she waits for the moon to rise

to the height of her window,
to the height of six tigers

which stare down her plantish body
yellow-eyed

from their place in the mural
nobody wanted.

She pauses, considers her options.

Watches them stare down
the baby-throat world,
bare their teeth.

REALITY

There is no belonging like this belonging,
there is no unity like this stink beetle—

you crush it and think of a balcony,
of a man, then you stop thinking.

There is another man, daily,
on the water, on a kayak,
the kind of man

who sees a bird's nest on your crown,
not a halo—a place to crawl into.

You'd like to crawl inside that nest, too.
You'd like someone who leaves
and then comes back, someone capable
of reconfiguration.

Instead you chew
your own dinner in the sun

and return to your crossword—
two down, seven letters for God.

SOURDOUGH

Quiet is the gift you give yourself
It keeps your day soft and alive
Nobody calls you

NERVE SIGNALS

I hope someone has noticed
my status update

We press our foreheads together
under the covers

I say, *I hope you're not trying too hard*

Though I kind of like it
when he tries too hard

The cucumbers have lost
their structural integrity

My husband's girlfriend
says he's a typical Aries

All the people I've ghosted
are haunting me

You'll know I love you when
I text you bedhead selfies

THIRSTY

I read about cults, take a narcissism quiz.
Not a narcissist: vain. Not a narcissist: exhibitionist.
Agree or disagree: *I like my body.*

I've been to self-love seminars run by three different Cathys
so yes, I like it, this soft meat thing.

Of course I'm not a charismatic leader of anyone,
only a soul with the option to spread legs, sing.

You can sit beside me. My attention's a bargain—
I'm just an animal that loves itself,
that loves you.

I DROPPED THEM ALL

This life: the juggler's palm.
Look at the ball. It cascades back and forth,
back and forth, left to right.

That's it. And then you add another.

Some people can juggle ten or fifteen balls,
some ninety. Some can juggle an elephant.

Juggle one ball you can juggle a thousand.

A giraffe, an armchair, a blue whale, a fountain.
Any other body, any other being,
a washed-up starfish, faceless.

That's all there is: a universe of bodies,
back and forth in palms.

FREEZE

There is a picture of me standing, my legs V-ed,
looking at a heron in her stream.

The heron is regal because of her long legs.
In the picture, she looks impossible.

My consciousness is floating
six inches from my crown.

I'm starved for meaning.
Can you eat a moment?

If I take this image—
something theoretical, something
not even hold-able—

if I take it and show it to somebody else,
then it becomes real.

What is real is taking the unreal,
turning it over like a fish, swallowing.

I'D SAY THINGS ARE NOW SUFFICIENTLY ABSURD

A harpoon harpoons a second harpoon and the Captain pulls on his pants. It's a gun, a knife, a pleasure. It's puddle of dead bees. A man stands: Who's in the bathroom? A man takes in an object with his eye, an eye like a harpoon, a harpoon eye. Below deck, I ask the Captain how he steers around the institutions, which bob above the surface like whimpering icebergs. My body eats itself for dinner while Cook fries up octopus. One leg at a time, the Captain says. Like everybody else.

TRAUMA PANORAMA

1.

Your maiden aunt kept every scrap of paper.
Every scrap. Sometimes she went to the movies.

When you're a maiden, your day unfolds like a horoscope.

You're a Capricorn, but don't let it distract you.
You keep being born at the centre of things.

2.

Did your parents ever lock you in a closet?
Is a part of you still locked inside a closet?

We don't want you to come out.
Some doors shouldn't be opened.

Meet another person, that person is you.
Meet a goldfinch. It's all projection.

3.

Pan is a ghost. He's in the closet with you.
He stomps his hooves at the scent of you.

Pan's eyes are amber marbles in your mouth.

He places a ticket stub on the surface of your tongue.
You bite down, and the door flies open.

IT'S THE SMALL THINGS THAT SAVE US

There is a button in the forest moss growing through a button which fell off a man's jacket a man's jacket in the forest is buttonless look at this caraway seed does it tell you something does the meadow tell you the tenderest mosses erect themselves a tower of buttons which fall as the spiders' legs reach out to ghosts leave dimes and men leave buttons spheres and rods men rip off elaborate buttons there are spaces in the forest a circle cast by biological cells emerging pollen bursting into fragrant bloom and the buttons hold everything together I like a nice brown button I like a space for my foot to land a softness a button leads me forward and to my left is everything and to my right is a nice soft deer who chews leaves her eyes are made for danger we don't get to decide a path of holy buttons the button pops off I lean against a tree and think about ants my skin is sticky and white I am useful my body covers a patch of dirt which now has coolness there is no part of me that wants to be explained an existence not slotted is a colony and a beetle takes a step into mud slippery hallways buttons scattered eyes deer eaten by a wolf and there is blood and under each fingernail a scraping under each fingernail a tiny world of my own making you hide in the holy shadow of tiny souls and millions of bacteria love you

ACKNOWLEDGEMENTS

Versions of some of these poems were published in my chapbook *HELLO NICE MAN* (Anstruther Press, 2019).

Thanks to the editors at *Room Magazine*, *THIS Magazine*, *The Fiddlehead*, *Contemporary Verse 2*, *Minola Review*, *Cathexis Northwest Press*, *Untethered Magazine*, *Literary Mama* and *Mortar Magazine*, where some poems in this collection first appeared.

Thanks to the Canada Council for the Arts for their generous support, and to my teachers at UBC—Ian Williams, Doretta Lau, Charlotte Gill, Maureen Medved, Nancy Lee and Susan Musgrave—for their mentorship and kindness.

Thanks to my other teachers, Alessandra Naccarato and Miranda Hill and Elisabeth de Mariaffi, and to all those who have written with me around my kitchen table.

Thanks to Jim Johnstone for making this book with me—I couldn't ask for a better editor.

Thanks to all the humans I love, especially my daughter.

ABOUT THE AUTHOR

Jaclyn Desforges is a Pushcart-nominated poet and the author of a picture book, *Why Are You So Quiet?* (Annick Press, 2020). She's the winner of the 2018 RBC/PEN Canada New Voices Award, two 2019 Short Works Prizes, and the 2020 Hamilton Emerging Artist Award for Writing. Jaclyn's work has been featured in *Room Magazine, THIS Magazine, The Fiddlehead, The Puritan, Contemporary Verse 2* and others. Currently, she works on the editorial board of the *Hamilton Review of Books* as Poetry Reviews Editor, and is a creative writing MFA candidate at the University of British Columbia. She lives in Hamilton, Ontario with her partner and daughter.